It was a sloth.

DELIVERY

Deliver to
Zzzzzoo
37 Zoo Street

It took a long time for the zoomkeepers to get the sloth out of the truck.

First they had to wake her up.

Then she needed a sip of water. . .

and a bit of a stretch, too.

When she finally looked around,
the sloth was perplexed.
You see, she thought her new
home would be pretty laid-back.

But this was the Zoom, not the Zzzzzoo.

At the Zoom, the zebras galloped so fast
they left their stripes in puddles.

The monkeys climbed so
fast they forgot to stop
at the treetops.

And the parrots flew so
fast their tails drew
rainbows across the sky.

What's all this
fuss and flutter
about?

wondered
the sloth.

After a few weeks, the sloth was
ready to make a new friend.

Can't stop now!

the monkeys screeched.

We're running ever so late!

They raced up and down and round and round the jungle gym.

The sloth shrugged her shaggy shoulders.
Then she chose a comfy spot where the
sun's golden rays would tickle her belly
all day long.

A few weeks after that, the sloth flagged down the zebras as they zipped by.

I like...

. . .your stripes,

she called.

They whinnied their thanks without stopping.

The sloth sighed.
She shook her shaggy head.

No one here
has any time.

Quite so,

a voice replied.

The sloth looked up.
Nothing.

The sloth looked down.

There, cupped in a philodendron
leaf, was a snail.

When the sloth arrived
at the snail's leaf, they
shared a bite.

Then they shared
a cool drink.

And as the setting sun
adorned the sky, they
shared a contented sigh.

The monkeys swung over.

What are you doing?

Sloth offered them some iced tea.

Next came the cheetah.

What's going on?

Snail offered her a sweet, green leaf to nibble on.

Mind if we join you?

asked the zebras.

Everyone shuffled to make some room.

And as day became night
and night became day, the animals
at the Zoom slowed down. . .

. . .just long enough, that is,
to become fast friends.

For the world's slowpokes, dawdlers, and lazybones.
Go ahead—take another nap. —HB

For my two favorite little monkeys. For all our crazy
(and lazy) moments. —O

Text © 2018 Helaine Becker
Illustrations © 2018 Orbie
First printing in paperback, 2021

Owlkids Books acknowledges the financial support of the Canada Council for the Arts, the Ontario Arts Council, the Government of Canada through the Canada Book Fund (CBF) and the Government of Ontario through the Ontario Creates Book Initiative for our publishing activities.

Published in Canada by
Owlkids Books Inc.
1 Eglinton Avenue East
Toronto, ON M4P 3A1

Published in the United States by
Owlkids Books Inc.
1700 Fourth Street
Berkeley, CA 94710

Library and Archives Canada Cataloguing in Publication

Title: Sloth at the zoom / Helaine Becker, Orbie.
Names: Becker, Helaine, author. | Orbie, 1984- illustrator.
Description: Written by Helaine Becker; illustrated by Orbie. | Originally published: Toronto, ON ;
   Berkeley, CA : Owlkids Books, ©2018.
Identifiers: Canadiana 2020040170X | ISBN 9781771474849 (softcover)
Classification: LCC PS8553.E295532 S66 2021 | DDC jC813/.6—dc23

Library of Congress Control Number: 2017961368

Edited by Jennifer MacKinnon
Designed by Danielle Arbour and Alisa Baldwin

ONTARIO ARTS COUNCIL
CONSEIL DES ARTS DE L'ONTARIO
an Ontario government agency
un organisme du gouvernement de l'Ontario

Canada Council
for the Arts

Conseil des Arts
du Canada

Canadä

Manufactured in Shenzhen, Guangdong, China, in April 2021, by WKT Co. Ltd.
Job #20CB2903

C   D   E   F   G   H

Publisher of Chirp, Chickadee and OWL
www.owlkidsbooks.com

Owlkids Books is a division of bayard canada